Parents and teachers—for a special note see page 32.

Also Available

3 abridged board book versions for ages 0–4

Where Is God?

What Does God Look Like?

How Does God Make Things Happen?

Because Nothing Looks Like God

BY **LAWRENCE KUSHNER** AND **KAREN KUSHNER**

ILLUSTRATED BY **DAWN W. MAJEWSKI**

Where is God?

God is in the beginning.

In the first red ripening tomato,

And in cookies fresh from the oven.

In the first fun day of vacation,

And in the tiny hands of a baby.

Where is God?

God is in the end.

In the last sweet bite of birthday cake,

And in your worn, torn baby blanket.

In the last wave good-bye at the end of a visit,

And in the closing moments of someone's life.

Where is God?

God is in the way people come together.

In the sharing of a cold and gloomy morning,

And in the Band-Aid fix-up after a fall.

In homemade gifts made of clay and paint,

And in morning hugs and goodnight kisses.

Where is God?

God is in the world.

In birdchirp, frogsong and chattering squirrels,

And in the fly caught in the spider's web.

In caterpillars chewing leaves from daisies,

And in worms turning leaves into earth.

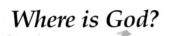

Where is God?

God is everywhere, if we only look.

God is wherever we let God in.

What does God look like?

God looks like nothing.

And nothing looks like God.

But there are many things you cannot see,

And still we are sure they are there.

Like cool breezes on a hot summer night,

Or the rays of the sun drying puddles of rain.

Like the long hours until suppertime,

Or the short minutes of a day at the beach.

You know they are there,

But there is nothing to see.

Like the kindness in someone's voice,

Or the happiness in a song.

Like the pride when Mom or Dad helps in your class,

Or the jumpy excitement at the start of a holiday.

You know it's there, but there is nothing to see.

Like the love your mom adds to your goodnight story,

Or your dad's hooray when you first tie your shoes.

Like your hope when it's your turn at bat,

Or your worry when your dog runs away.

You know it's there,

But there is nothing to see.

God doesn't look like anything either,

Because there is nothing to see.

But everyone and everything gives us clues that God is here.

Clues that point to the One we cannot see.

How does God make things happen?

Look at your family.

See sisters taking turns on the slide,

And brothers sharing a new game.

Watch how everyone comes

together to help with dinner.

How does God make things happen?

Look at your school.

A boy helps when another can't reach.

A girl shares her lunch.

Watch how everyone shows the swings

to a new friend.

How does God make things happen?

Look at your town.

One family gives money for

people who lost their home.

A neighborhood gathers books

for children in the hospital.

Watch how everyone helps a

family with a new baby.

To Papa Charlie, who reads stories to us
—L.K. & K.K.
To the creative light shining in all us children
—D.W.M.

Because Nothing Looks Like God

2003 Third Printing
2001 Second Printing
2000 First Printing
Text © 2000 by Lawrence Kushner and Karen Kushner
Illustrations © 2000 by Jewish Lights Publishing

For information regarding permission to reprint material from this book, please mail or fax your request in writing to Jewish Lights Publishing, Permissions Department, at the address / fax number listed below, or e-mail your request to permissions@jewishlights.com.

Library of Congress Cataloging-in-Publication Data
Kushner, Lawrence, 1943–
Because nothing looks like God / by Lawrence Kushner and Karen Kushner ; illustrated by Dawn Majewski.
p.   cm.
ISBN 1-58023-092-X (hc.)
1. God—Juvenile literature. [1. God.] I. Kushner, Karen, 1946– II. Majewski, Dawn, ill. III. Title.
BL473.K87 2000
291.2'11—dcx21
00-009625

10 9 8 7 6 5 4 3

Manufactured in China
Book and jacket design: Bronwen Battaglia

For People of All Faiths, All Backgrounds
Published by Jewish Lights Publishing
A Division of LongHill Partners, Inc.
Sunset Farm Offices, Route 4, P.O. Box 237
Woodstock, VT 05091
Tel: (802) 457-4000   Fax: (802) 457-4004
www.jewishlights.com

FOR PARENTS AND TEACHERS

This book addresses the kind of religious questions that small children have but are often unable to put into words. Hearing about God in church, synagogue, or mosque can be very confusing and often leaves children with basic questions unanswered. With *Because Nothing Looks Like God*, parents and children can share and explore the questions and answers together, in an open, creative way.

Instead of offering dogmatic answers, this book suggests ways for children to be aware of God's presence in a way that helps them to lay down the foundation of what will become a mature adult spiritual world-view.

Too much of children's religious literature is meant to be outgrown. But just because children's cognitive development makes some theological ideas difficult (or impossible) for them to comprehend does not excuse us from telling as much of the truth as possible. For this reason these stories talk about matters of the spirit without anthropomorphizing God or asking a child to believe things that he or she will later discard and replace.

"Where Is God?" opens the possibility that God is present not only in vacations and new babies but also in spiders and death. This encourages a conversation where children can express their own awareness of God and realize that different people find God in different places.

"What Does God Look Like?" addresses the question of God's existence that troubles young concrete thinkers: How do you know about something that cannot be seen? By providing examples of things they already know exist but are not visible, this section helps children to realize that we know about things in many different ways. It encourages them to become detectives who collect clues of God's presence in the world.

"How Does God Make Things Happen?" suggests that God does not dramatically intervene in the world except through the use of human hands. Being a part of God's activities in the world is an appealing idea to small children who enjoy feeling powerful but have few opportunities. The idea of using one's power for the betterment of the community allows every child to be a real superhero.

Above all, *Because Nothing Looks Like God* is a starting place—the beginning of a continuing conversation between adults and children about the world and God.